Other Madness Heart Press Books featuring Lucas Mangum:

- Mania
- Extinction Peak
- The MHP Employee Handbook
- Bladejob

Madness Heart Press
2006 Idlewilde Run Dr.
Austin, Texas 78744

reviously published as "Primitive" in Horrorama, published by Grindhouse Press, 2020

A MHP Pocket Book
www.madnessheart.press

Bestial

by Lucas Mangum

A Madness Heart Press Pocket Book

Editor's Note

The pages that follow were found among the belongings of a Professor Walton Roberts, who disappeared somewhere in the Tatoosh Wilderness near the town of Paradise, Washington, along with his three companions: programmer Bryan Hobbs, professional mover Hank Sullivan, and corporate banker Tony Tabs. Along with these papers, authorities discovered remains of an illegal campsite, and an RV registered to Tabs was found abandoned on the outskirts of Paradise. Additionally, evidence suggests the missing men may have engaged in the illicit killings of several wolves in the area. As of this writing, no other trace of these four men has been uncovered. It has also been speculated their disappearance is somehow tied to a series of nearby child murders and the vanishing of a Ms. Luca Barath, whose own son was a suspect in the killings. However, no evidence linking these tragedies has ever been found.

Moon Mountain

We loaded up Tony's RV on Thursday evening. It was Memorial Day weekend. The semester was over, Tony and Bryan had taken off from their jobs, and Hank had been laid off again. The stars had aligned perfectly. I had five whole days away from it all. Five days with my high school buddies. Men I hadn't seen in almost fifteen years. For most of those fifteen years, we talked about doing something like this, but nothing materialized until now. It couldn't have come at a better time either. Not for me, anyway.

I'd just lost custody of my son, Wiley. Apparently, my ex-wife and the judge she was fucking determined my drinking was a detriment to my parenting. Never mind I only drank at night. Never mind I didn't black out. Never mind I still held down my tenured position at California State University's Department of History. Of course, Ayla was a good lay. That probably had some bearing on the Honorable Alexander Smart's ruling. Not that I could prove anything was going on. Anyway, I planned to get my son back, but first, I needed some time away. Four nights in the Tatoosh Range should do the trick.

As we packed the RV with supplies, Tony's wife made barbecue short ribs and mashed potatoes. His twin daughters chased the family German shepherd around the expansive front lawn. The sun was setting too fast, but I tried not to think about it. We hadn't planned this trip so I could worry about time.

When we finished, the seven of us sat down to one of the best meals I'd had in years. I felt like a man who'd just gotten out of prison. It took all I had not to devour the food in an embarrassingly short amount of time. Ayla was a shit cook, not like Tony's wife, Yvette, at all. That wasn't the only way they differed. Ayla had small tits and practically no ass. She was pasty-faced, and her hair was damaged from frequent dyeing. Yvette, on the other hand, was thick where it counted, dark-skinned, and her hair was a nest of sensuous braids.

Tony Tabs had a good life. Though he had grown up in the same low-income cesspool as the rest of us, he'd turned out okay. He was Vice President of Corporate Banking at a Sacramento financial institution. He had a house in El Dorado Hills, two beautiful twin girls, and an obedient but intimidating dog. Plus, he got to nail Yvette whenever he wanted. I wasn't jealous of him or anything, but sometimes I wished my life was as sweet. It was nice of him to share the wealth this weekend.

After dinner, Tony and Yvette put the girls to bed while Bryan, Hank, and I sat on the back deck drinking High West Campfire Whiskey. Bryan did most of the talking. Found out after college he was into dicks, which was fine, long as he didn't touch mine. One high school experience aside, I just wasn't into gay shit.

On this night, while Hank and I watched the stars and moon come out, Bryan went on about how welcoming the tech world was to people like him. He talked about his three cats: an orange tabby named Eva; a gray and white domestic shorthair named Jack; and Oliver, who looked like he was crossbred with a skunk in all his pictures. He said he wasn't dating anyone seriously but was still having fun and not exactly ready to settle down. I nodded here and there and told him that was good. Hank didn't say shit. I always thought he might be a bit homophobic. Just a bit, though. I mean, he wouldn't have stayed friends with us if it bothered him that much. Of course, maybe he had nothing against gay men at all. Maybe he was just quiet because, like me, he was also recently divorced and having no fun being single, whereas Bryan seemed to be enjoying himself. Either way, I think we were all ready to hit the road.

Tony came outside with a big grin on his face. "You guys save enough Campfire for me?"

"Sure, man, you got a glass?" Hank asked and proffered the bottle.

Tony waved it away. "Kidding. Since it's my rig, I'll drive first. Give you guys a chance to sober up."

"I'm sober," Bryan said. "Perfectly sober."

"With you, I could never tell," Tony said. "You've only ever had one gear."

"I can drive if you need me to," Bryan said.

"Nah, I'd rather start us out." Tony opened his palm to show us the keys. "Finish those shots, boys. We got a lot of miles ahead."

Tony went inside. Hank grimaced as he knocked back the remnants of his booze. I held my nose and did the same. Bryan had no trouble putting the rest of the whiskey down. He slammed his glass on the nearest tabletop and nodded. We all got up and followed Tony through the house. At the front door, Yvette hugged all of us. She lingered on me and told me to take care of Tony. I told her I would, and then she released me and gave Tony a goodbye kiss. I tried not to stare, but the slurp of their tongues was hard to ignore.

Hank sat up front with Tony. Bryan lay down on one of the RV's built-in beds. I sat all the way in the back to try writing something. I'd told myself I'd get some writing done on this trip. Unfortunately, I had no idea where to start. It'd been a while since I'd written fiction. I couldn't even remember the last time I'd tried. Though I still sometimes called myself a novelist, I'd only published one book when I was in my mid-twenties. A mystery novel called *The Hangman's Gambit*. It'd done okay, but not good enough to launch my career. Turned out I was better suited for academics.

Still, something inside me yearned for release. Maybe another book. But it felt more primal than that, like inside of me lay a dormant monster caged by modern society, more specifically, caged by me, who was deceived by modern society's perceived treasures. I sometimes thought maybe this same sleeping hunger dwelled in all of us, but Tony seemed pretty content, Bryan too. Even Hank, through simplification forced upon him by poverty, maybe had it figured out. Maybe they were lying. That was always possible. Or maybe they were still riding a high and hadn't come down yet. Either way, they were different from me. I was aware of this monster. Sometimes I was so aware, I felt like it would tear itself out of me.

The drive from El Dorado Hills to Paradise,

Washington, is somewhere between twelve and thirteen hours. We made good time by driving in shifts and peeing in the RV's bathroom. We reached Rainier National Park around eight in the morning, local time. I was last to drive, and I parked us in the common lot. The four of us split the cost of parking, as if we fully intended on camping where we were allowed. As soon as I got out of the RV, I noticed a difference in the air. It was so much cleaner than city air but somehow also more textured. As well as its damp, earthy quality, I detected the sweet, strong smell of the evergreen and the smokiness of nearby campfires. I already felt much better.

From the lot, we hiked up to Moon Mountain and wandered from the trail when we were sure no one was around to notice. Only the trees watched. They stood all around us like many-limbed sentries, decked in myriad shades of green and capable of only swaying. Tony said he knew where he was going. We all just went along with it. In a clearing on the side of the mountain, we set up camp. Tony and Hank got a fire going. I gathered stumps and stones for us to sit on. Bryan grilled up some meat patties he'd formed and seasoned back home. We ate them on sesame buns with spicy mustard and American cheese. Afterwards, we sat around the fire. Tony broke out the whiskey. We sat, silent.

Tony opened his backpack and dug out several items I, at first, couldn't identify. As he began to snap the pieces together, I realized what they were. What the pieces made up.

"You brought your gun?" Hank said, beating me to the punch.

Tony grinned. "Didn't you, white boy?"

"Nah, I had to sell mine a while back."

Without getting up, Tony dragged the bag over to Hank. "Lucky for you, I brought an extra." Hank immediately started rooting through the bag for the other disassembled rifle. Tony nodded toward Bryan and me. "What about you two?"

"I brought this," Bryan said, patting the machete sheathed on the side of his bag.

"I didn't bring anything larger than a buck knife," I said. I neglected to mention that for the last three years, I'd written numerous letters advocating for stricter gun laws and campaigned against animal cruelty.

Tony nodded and kept putting the gun together. When he finished, he racked it and turned to look me at me, eyes blazing but features otherwise unmoving.

"Seen you looking at my wife back there," he said.

I sniffed. My eyes shifted. My brain fumbled for something to say.

"No need denying it. No need to be ashamed either. She's a fine piece of woman."

"Yeah," I croaked.

"You want her?"

"What?"

"You heard me."

"Well, I . . ."

I felt myself shrink inside. This was gonna get bad. I held his gaze, though. Even with that gun in Tony's hands, I didn't want to show him, or the others, any signs of weakness. I licked my lips but had no spit. I blinked. He started laughing. The others joined him, albeit shakily. I tried to grin but imagined I was grimacing. The laughter died down.

"Just fucking with you, man. What happened

with you and yours anyhow?"

I shrugged. "Didn't work out, I guess."

Hank finished his shot and poured himself another.

"Come on, man. Gotta be more to the story than that. She fuck around on you?" Tony asked.

"I don't know."

Tony raised his eyebrows. "You fuck around on her?"

"No! No, we just grew apart. That's all."

Tony eyed me another few seconds. It felt like a full minute. Finally, he nodded. "That's some shit."

I drank the rest of my shot and relished its burn. Then I poured another.

"Yeah," I said. "Yeah, that's some shit."

We all went silent again for a while. Hank broke it by saying he was glad we finally got to do this. We finished our whiskey and retired to our tents to nap for a little. No one had really done much sleeping during the drive. An hour or two of shuteye would do us some good. I didn't sleep, though. I lay awake with a large rock pressing into my lower back. I thought about Tony asking me if I wanted to fuck his wife. Tony with his immovable gaze. Tony with his rifle. I thought I'd hear that weapon cocking the rest of my life.

I'd been friends with him the longest. He'd been on the football team, but once that season ended, he ran indoor and outdoor track. Had we gone to different schools, we'd have been fierce rivals. Since we were on the same team, our competition stayed friendly. We were constantly trying to outdo each other. Sometimes, my time would be better. Other times, he'd outpace me. In tenth grade, he invited me to a party with his football teammates. The cops had shown up, and the two of us escaped together, running like mad through an open field and ducking into a patch of woods, trying to hold in our laughter as flashlight beams scanned the area. After that, we were inseparable until he left community college for business school. We'd stayed in contact, though, mostly through social media, where we watched each other settle into careers and suburban domesticity.

I wondered if he would've shot me earlier

had I answered his question about Yvette in the affirmative.

Nah, I thought. *Not Tony. He isn't a killer. None of us are.*

Even as I thought this, I reminded myself you can never really know anyone. A fact that had become all too clear during the dissolution of my marriage.

Not long after Wiley's birth, it dawned on me that though Ayla loved me, she didn't like me. I saw it in her eyes whenever we had people over and I'd go off about politics or religion. Usually, these rants came out after four or five drinks. When she and I met, we enjoyed debating these topics. She identified as Christian; I was spiritual, not religious. She considered herself a moderate Republican; I never voted. We came together on a few key things: first, we enjoyed these arguments; second, we had great sex; and third, we each thought the way we did because we cared about people.

As our relationship went on, she began to feel at odds with her party and we both started voting Democrat. Her because she'd evolved on several key issues like gay marriage, healthcare, and the environment. Me because if our country did implode, I wanted to be able to say, "Hey, I tried." Even though we came together on that, we drifted further apart on religion. I went full atheist while she became an active member of her church, which seemed to contradict her liberalizing, but that's Californian Christianity for you.

Our goals also held us together those first few years. I pursued my doctorate in American History and worked on *The Hangman's Gambit* whenever I could. After she graduated, she opened her interior design business. We lived in a small apartment. Seeing each other sometimes proved difficult. Despite those drawbacks, we were each working toward things. We had our separate goals and our mutual goal of getting a house in the suburbs and having some kids. Sounds basic, I know, but short of going off to live in the woods like Thoreau, it was the only way we knew how to simplify without living somewhere small and unsafe. It was nice feeling like there was something ahead for both of us, individually and collectively.

During the last year of my doctorate, I got a book deal for *The Hangman's Gambit*. A medium-sized New York press paid a five-figure advance to publish the manuscript in trade and digital. I'd been told that shit never happened anymore. Guess I was told wrong. I got a job at California State. We bought a house, not in El Dorado Hills but in a decent neighborhood just the same. Ayla's business grew so much she hired on an assistant. Wiley came along about a year after we got settled in.

We did everything right and then some. The goddamn American Dream wasn't dead, and we were living proof. I should've known it was too fucking good to be true.

The Hangman's Gambit did not sell as well as expected. The run started out okay, but then some book blogger with a chip on her shoulder decided she didn't like how I portrayed women or minorities in my novel. And that was all it took to sink the book. I was a racist, misogynist prick, and probably also a secret Nazi. Never mind my straight White male characters were also dirtbags. Never mind my best friend was Black. Never mind I voted Democrat, donated to Planned Parenthood, and came out every year for the Women's March. Though my book wasn't outright banned or pulled, sales tanked so badly a second book contract was impossible.

I got depressed. Part of it might have been post-partum depression, which, it turned out, also affected dads. The book's failure was a huge factor too, though. After all, I'd dreamed of being a professional writer since I was seven years old. I'd been denied, maybe forever. Other factors were in play too, of course. During her pregnancy, Ayla had stopped drinking and maintained her sobriety after Wiley's birth. I did not, and after the book failed, I started drinking a lot more. Add to that the fact that giving birth had completely annihilated Ayla's sex drive and you had a perfect storm of frustrated, drunken misery.

I wanted something. Not just sex or money or success as a writer. I wanted that unattainable *something* I believed we all wanted, something that couldn't even be put into words. You could call it spiritual, but that word's been so cheapened over time, I felt dirty using it. My nighttime drives through dark, winding roads made that something feel close. So did getting so drunk I loosened my tongue and vented all my frustration to Ayla, who simply told me to try seducing her or getting a second job or writing another book. Most of all, she said I should slow down on my drinking.

"We have a kid now," was her mantra.

Maybe she'd been right about all those things. Still, she never made it seem like she *wanted* to be seduced. A second job would keep me from being a more present father. Writing another book was impossible; that book blogger had forever tarnished my name. I told Ayla all this, but she never listened. It always came back to my drinking. She could do no wrong. I felt more alone than any married man should feel.

I never cheated, though. Don't get me wrong, I came close many times. Getting propositioned by hot young students. The times I went to bars and noticed my type of woman looking lonesome. The time Wiley's babysitter had me pick her up from a party that had gotten out of control: she'd asked me not to tell her parents and said she'd do *anything* to repay me.

Through all this, I stayed faithful. Sometimes this meant I had to beat my dick in the shower.

No, I didn't cheat; she did. I should've known something was fishy. Woman never worked out a day in her life, and all of a sudden, she started caring about her figure. Weight training, cardio, kickboxing. You name it, she did it, or at least tried it. I ignored the voice in my head telling me she was doing this to attract another mate. Even when nights she left me to handle Wiley's routine became more frequent. Even when I met her trainer: a man so gorgeous, even I considered switching teams. Even when I saw the outright disdain in her eyes whenever we had company and I was on one of my rants. Granted, I was usually shit-bombed in the latter scenario and likely being obnoxious, but I didn't think it warranted such a glare. Sometimes I thought she outright hated me.

But no, there wasn't someone else. Couldn't be. She wasn't a cheater.

But she was. I guess I didn't know her like I thought I did.

Maybe I didn't know myself either.

I can't decide which is worse.

I miss Wiley.

After our naps, we shared some trail mix and went on a hike. There's nothing like mountain air. It has a crispness, a purity that air closer to sea level just doesn't have. And city air, forget it. There's no comparison. Breathing in and out as we hiked made me feel a long-forgotten vitality. I felt truly pure. *Honest.* And the view. *Goddamn.* Peaks and trees for endless miles. I considered taking some photos, but I couldn't stand to distill these sights in any way, shape, or form. This was for me and only for this moment.

I didn't share any of this with my companions. Instead, I joined them in talking about pussy. Hank talked about the occasional white trash babe he picked up at his local watering hole. Tony, unsurprisingly, talked about his encounters with his lovely wife. I kept my stories relegated to women I'd fucked before I met Ayla and embellished tales of women I'd met since the divorce. Bryan said his only experience with pussy was a sexual assault in which a woman in a miniskirt took off her panties and sat on his face while he was sleeping.

"Shit, I wish I'd get assaulted like that," Hank said.

"Yeah, me too," I muttered.

"A woman would only do that to a man she knew was gay," Hank said.

Tony grinned. "Sometimes Yvette will do that to me."

"When you're sleeping?" I asked.

He shrugged one shoulder. "We have an agreement."

"An agreement?"

He laughed, a rich and mischievous sound, but he didn't elaborate. Looking at him in the afternoon light, I recognized, not for the first time, why he'd managed to get so far. He had a way about him. He carried himself with a confidence seldom seen outside the world of professional sports. He had a winning smile. A body just as toned, if not more so, than it'd been in high school. He embodied tall, dark, and handsome. I recognized these were odd thoughts for a straight man to have, but I had them just the same. Dude was charming.

"Ick," Bryan said. "You guys are gonna make me vomit."

He said it in a classic gay guy lisp he didn't have back when I knew him in high school.

"Does some switch in your head that makes you talk like that get flipped when you come out of the closet?" I asked.

"Oh-ho, shit," Tony said, covering his mouth as he laughed.

Hank laughed too, but also tried to hide it.

"You know that's offensive, right?" Bryan asked. "I mean, you can't be that dense."

Heat filled my face. "I mean, yeah, but I guess . . . I, um . . . sorry."

"Hey, we're all friends here, right?" Tony said.

"Hard to argue with the man with a gun," Bryan said. "But no, I'm not mad or anything. Just, you know, try to think before you talk. Maybe speak with the tact you show in your writing."

"So you've read my stuff?" I asked.

"Of course. I didn't think your book was offensive either. You just tried to be real."

"I appreciate that," I said. "Really."

"We're friends."

I almost dug deeper after that comment. Was that the only reason he liked the book? Or defended it? I itched to know, but at my age, you learn showing such insecurity is improper, so I stayed quiet.

We hiked on. Some miles later, we circled back so we could reach camp by sundown. When we arrived, Tony and Hank restarted the fire. I helped Bryan dish out some chicken salad and pour more whiskey. Seated around the fire, we ate in relative silence. Occasionally, Hank burped. The fire crackled. The sky turned orange, then purple, then black. All four of us perked up at the sound of nearby howling.

"The hell was that?" Hank said. "Coyote?"

"Nah," Tony said. "Sounded bigger. Wolves."

"There are wolves in Washington?" Bryan asked.

"Shit yeah, there are," Tony said. "Wanna go hunting?"

At this, my guts clenched.

Hank said, "I don't know, man. I might be too drunk."

"You ain't had any more to drink than the

rest of us," Tony said.

"Yeah, but . . ." Hank drifted off, then shook his head. "Tolerance ain't what it used to be."

"Whatever you say, man," Tony said.

The wolves howled again. They sounded close. I wondered how close. Had to be damn near ten of them. I was starting to rethink my position on guns. Tony must have detected something because he slapped my arm.

"Hey, man. We leave them alone, they'll leave us alone. Right?"

I nodded. "Yeah, right."

"We should tell ghost stories," Bryan said. We all looked at him. "What? It could be fun."

"You know any ghost stories?" Tony asked.

"I know a few," Hank said.

Now we all turned to Hank.

"Bet you do," Tony said. "Bet you seen some shit."

"I have."

"So, let's hear it. Spook us."

Hank looked down. He seemed to be considering something.

"What are you waiting for?"

"Trying to think of one that isn't so damn

depressing."

At this, we all laughed. Not only had Hank seen some shit, we knew he'd been through some shit. I remembered a selfie he took the day he got out of rehab a few years back. He'd captioned it, *Drugs kicked my ass, but they can't kill me, I'm still here.* Opiates had been his drug of choice. Apparently, pain pills were a hot commodity in the moving business. I wondered if he was even supposed to be drinking alcohol with us, but he hadn't said otherwise, so I figured it best not to ask.

"All right, got something." We all leaned in to listen. "My Uncle Davey was a bartender in Hollywood Hills. Got all sorts of characters coming in for drinks and chatter. The strangest, though, he told me, was a man that went by the name Mr. Boggs. According to my uncle, the man was always on about religion and black magic and communing with the devil. Just weird shit you don't say in public unless there's something off about you. The hell of it was, though, this Mr. Boggs didn't seem crazy. He was well-spoken, calm and collected. He was always well-groomed and dressed in expensive suits. The only thing that wasn't quite right was the way he smelled. Uncle Davey said the man always smelled like he'd been sitting next to a fire."

"Kinda like we are now," Bryan said.

"Guess so, maybe. Maybe not. Anyway, one of these nights, this Mr. Boggs asks Uncle Davey to come with him to some kind of meeting where he and his friends were going to contact Satan. Now, Uncle Davey was a Roman Catholic, so séances and satanic rituals were off limits. Naturally, he tells Mr. Boggs no but wishes him luck. Even tells the strange man he'll pray for him. To this, Boggs only smiled lightly without showing any teeth. My uncle used the word 'ironic' to describe Boggs's smile. Without another word, Mr. Boggs leaves.

"Now, Mr. Boggs was a regular at this point. Came in something like three times a week. But after that night, he stopped coming. Every time someone came in on one of these regular nights, Uncle Davey glanced up, expecting to see the weirdo. But he never does. On Uncle Davey's off nights, he wonders if Boggs is simply avoiding him, and he starts asking the other bartenders if they've seen Boggs. All of them say no.

"Something like a month goes by. Uncle Davey starts to forget about Boggs. But then one night, Boggs is already there when Uncle Davey comes in for his shift. Boggs looks up and grins at Uncle Davey. This time, he shows teeth. Uncle Davey told me he still sees that grin every time he has a nightmare. I should probably mention that—to this day—Uncle Davey can't tell this story without sobbing like a little baby. I've seen him tell it plenty of times. By the end of it, he's always a blubbering mess.

"Anyway, he goes behind the bar and asks Mr. Boggs if he needs a refill. Boggs says, 'That won't be necessary, I just wanted to give you these.' And he hands my uncle a stack of photographs. Then he leaves without another word. My uncle starts looking through the photographs. The first picture shows a large hill from a distance. The details aren't so great. A second photo is again of the hill, but this time, the one taking the picture is standing closer. The hill has what my uncle calls a 'sinewy' quality. Says it almost has the quality of captured motion. But like the first photo, this one has a gray tint to it; it's not quite black and white, but it's close. Because of that, it's still hard to make out what he's looking at.

"He looks at the third photo. The hill is closer now. He's not sure, but he thinks the sinewy bulges are people all laid down on the hill. And it looks like someone's standing over all of them. Also, there's a ravine or some kind of large winding tube going from the top of the hill to the bottom, and the people lying on the hill are . . . gathered around it somehow. The fourth photo, the man at the top of the hill is in focus. He's got a face my uncle describes as . . . fuck, what was that word? Oh, yeah. 'Bestial.' Like, wild or animal-like, I think."

"That's right," I said.

Hank held my gaze, then nodded. This didn't feel like story time anymore. Something about this story gave me the creeps. I bet the others felt it too. All of us were at the literal edges of our seats, staring wide-eyed at Hank, who'd lost all the color in his face. His features now looked drawn and wasted.

"The man-beast in the photo was very short,

a midget, basically. But the winding tubular thing turns out to be his . . . well, his dick." The three of us listening sat up straight. "And the people are reaching for it with their hands and . . . and their mouths.

"He flips to the next photo, and this is when Davey usually loses it when telling this story. He flips to the next photo, and the people laid across the hill are now in focus. They're his fucking family members. *My* fucking family members. He sees his wife and kids. His parents and grandparents. My parents. My other uncles and aunts. My cousins. Me. We're all either teething on this midget devil's massive cock or caressing it. Uncle Davey says all our eyes are glazed and rolled back like we're on some kind of heavy drug, or like we're, you know, coming."

Bryan laughed out loud.

Hank shot him a glare. "Hey, fuck you. This is my goddamn family."

"I'm sorry, Hank," Bryan said. "What are you saying? Your family's cursed?"

Hank shrugged. "Feels like it sometimes."

"Ah, that's bullshit, man," Tony said. "You

skipped college and went straight to work. Didn't bother making yourself marketable. Can't blame that on Satan."

"Almost everyone in my family has struggled with substance abuse. Most of us die young, except Uncle Davey, weirdly enough. It's like he's the one that's got to tell us."

"I'm sorry," Bryan said again. "That's just crazy."

Tony nodded toward me. "What do you think?"

"I think anything's possible," I said. "Most likely, though, Uncle Davey's probably mentally ill."

"Last time I tell you cocksuckers a ghost story," Hank said.

"Hey," Tony said, "we're just having a little fun, right? Anyone want to go next?"

Hank softened.

"I'll go," I said, and everyone turned to me.

I told them about something I stumbled upon during my research for *The Hangman's Gambit*. Like Hank's tale of the devil and his bartending uncle, mine was set in Hollywood. Unlike his story, though, mine boasted multiple sources. All of them were anonymous internet trolls, sure, but they all said pretty much the same thing. A girl named Marielle went to Hollywood with dreams of becoming a star. She fell in love with a famous director. Many names got thrown around in identifying this man, but Stephen Ward came up the most. She suffered tremendous abuse and, eventually, was killed by the guy, who wrote her story as a screenplay. Supposedly, anyone who tried to film this screenplay either died or went completely crazy. According to legend, the script wound up in the hands of Stephen's son William, who managed to set Marielle free, but it cost him and his girlfriend their lives. Crazy as the story was, all of these people were real. All of them had died under mysterious circumstances.

"I think I read a book about that," Bryan said. "It was called *Mania* or something."

"Whoa, really?" I said. I hadn't heard of it.

"Yeah, I forget the author's name, though."

"Was the book any good?" Hank asked.

"Eh, it was okay. Kinda fell apart in the third act."

"Most books do," I said. "Endings are hard."

"You managed to end yours pretty well," Bryan said.

"Thanks."

Bryan shrugged. "Don't mention it."

"Want to hear my story about the ghost of a bank teller?" Tony asked. At this, we all laughed. "Hey, I'm serious. He keeps the robbers away from his branch."

We all laughed harder. Tony joined us. When we all died down, we looked at Bryan.

"Whatchu got?" Tony asked.

"Nothing exciting, really."

"Wait, weren't you all about that paranormal shit back in school?" Hank asked.

"I was, but conspiracy theories just stopped being fun. That whole scene got co-opted by a bunch of rightwing nuts. Aliens and Bigfoot I can buy, but tell me the Holocaust was a hoax, you can fuck right off."

At this, we all nodded. We drank some more and fed the fire more logs. I looked up at the sky, tried counting the stars, and gave up before I even reached ten. With my whiskey buzz going, they were all doubling and tripling anyway. Even without that, the amount of visible stars completely dwarfed what I could see back in the city. I had a thought then about how more light only blinded you. There was some fundamental truth in that, but I was too drunk to put my finger on it. Story of my life.

Not that my drinking was really a problem. If I was an alcoholic, I was a high-functioning one. And if I was functioning, what did it matter? I guess Ayla figured it mattered. Somehow, she'd convinced Judge Smart it mattered too. I was a good father. Maybe I was a bad husband, but she wasn't exactly wife of the year either.

Tony backhanded me in the chest. I flashed a glare at him.

"You good?" he asked.

"Yeah, just thinking about shit."

"Well, that never did anyone any good," Hank said.

We all laughed. We poured another round. My head was gonna hurt like hell tomorrow, and I didn't give a shit. It was good to be there. Good to be with friends. Friends, real friends, felt more and more like a rarity the older I got. People wanted to get together but only if it somehow related to work or if their kids were the same age as yours. This was different. I looked back up at the stars again. This time, everything was slowly spinning. I felt my lips curve into a smile. I closed my eyes. I felt damn good.

Since we didn't pay much attention to time, I didn't know what time it was when I staggered back to my tent. All I knew was the spinning sensation was increasing. I didn't think I'd throw up, but I knew I was damn close. Good thing I stopped drinking when I did. As I lay at the edge of sleep, I thought about Hank's story of the midget devil's dick and Hank's family sucking it. I wished I could write something like that. The visceral response that story's strange imagery inspired rivaled anything I'd read in years and far eclipsed anything I'd ever written. I drifted deeper into slumber and tried to forget the awful story. I even tried praying to ward it off. I know that sounds crazy: a grown-ass man, an atheist at that, afraid of a stupid story, but sometimes, especially at the brink of sleep, the unreal seems so real knowing better doesn't mean shit. I lay there, bobbing up from the black sea of the unconscious, trying to forget the monsters that swam beneath its troubled surface. The sleep that finally took me was fitful and broken.

I woke up in the middle of the night. My bladder felt like a water balloon filled to full capacity. My brain felt like it was trapped inside a clenched fist. I croaked out a curse that scratched the back of my throat and propped myself on my elbows. Just outside, the fire had been reduced to glowing embers. Whoever had gone to sleep last had forgotten to douse it. If I remembered, I'd give a Smokey the Bear PSA tomorrow.

I moved with tremendous care. Everything hurt. Even the persistent chirping of crickets seemed oppressive. I didn't remember drinking *that* much, but maybe I had. Or maybe I hadn't gotten enough water during the day. I stepped past the dwindling fire and reminded myself to stay hydrated. There was water in my tent. I'd take a few gulps before going back to sleep. I reached the edge of the clearing, took out my dick with one hand, and wiped my eyes with the other. As I peed, I kept my eyes closed. Though I no longer had the spins, I feared they might come back. My piss sounded incredibly loud when it hit the dead leaves at my feet. When I finished, I shook dry best I could, put my dick away, and opened my eyes.

I was face to face with a goddamn wolf. Even though I knew I'd left my buck knife in the tent, I reached for my hip where it would've been anyway. Not that a knife would be much help against this monster. It was twice the size of Tony's German shepherd, which is to say it was fucking massive. Its eyes gleamed in the starlight. Its snout was wrinkled up into a silent snarl. If it started growling, I knew for sure I'd piss again, this time soaking my pajama pants. The wolf and I stared each other down. I wanted to look away because I was pretty sure meeting its gaze would be seen as a challenge, but I was afraid to move. I was afraid to speak. Even breathing seemed ill-advised. Despite reservations, I slid one foot back. The wolf glanced down to follow the motion with a glare. Now it did growl.

"Shit," I said.

The wolf bent its legs, prepared to pounce. Its white teeth shone like ivory daggers. I forgot my hangover even as my pulse throbbed like underwater explosions in my head. The growl of the beast grew louder, more timorous, which was worse: a scared animal is even more dangerous. I took another trembling step backwards. The wolf leaned all its weight back. It was going to jump on me any minute. Running would do me no good. By the time I turned, it'd be upon me, pinning me facedown and taking a bite out of the tense meat between my neck and shoulder.

Something exploded. The wolf yelped and dashed off to the side, scurrying away, fading into the black like a silver and gray ghost. I turned to see Tony with his rifle pointed up in the air. My mouth worked, trying to find the words to express some kind of gratitude, but I made no sound. He just nodded at me and went back to his tent. The throb of my hangover returned. So did the bone-deep exhaustion. Yeah, I'd be drinking less tomorrow. I padded back to my tent, gulped down a generous helping of water, and tried to sleep.

When I came out of my tent the next morning, my hangover had dulled. Everyone else was already awake. They looked at me and burst out laughing.

"You really show your dick to a wolf?" Hank said.

"I didn't know it was there."

"Divorce has made you a desperate man," Bryan said.

I gave him the finger and sat down on a stump. The fire was at full strength again. I remembered my intended spiel about putting it out before bed. I needed to wake up some more before I lectured anyone. Tony passed me a steaming mug of black coffee. I smelled it and took a sip.

"Fuck yeah, dude. Just what I needed."

"Something strong and black, huh?" he said and winked.

We all laughed about that one. Breakfast was eggs, home fries, and ham. We did some more hiking, ate salami and cheese sandwiches for lunch, talked about sex some more, gathered firewood, and spent time alone in our respective tents. I did some journaling and nodded out for a few minutes intermittently.

When evening rolled around again, Tony and Hank said they wanted to go on a wolf hunt. Since there wasn't really anything else to do, Bryan and I reluctantly agreed. We waited for total darkness and listened for the howling. It started up, and we headed toward it. The more we followed it, the farther off it seemed to get. But then it fell silent for a while and we stood still. We all looked to Tony, but he stayed pokerfaced, flexing his hands on his rifle's stock.

"Dude," Hank said, but Tony put up a hand to silence him.

My gaze flitted around the thick, dark woods. A sinking feeling overcame me. This was a terrible fucking idea. What the hell were we doing? As far as I knew, none of us were professional hunters. I sure as shit wasn't. If my three buddies' Facebook pages were anything to go off of, neither were they. I opened my mouth to suggest going back but closed it again when the howling resumed. From the sound of it, the wolves were all around us and very close by.

"We should split up," Tony said.

"Are you nuts?" Bryan asked.

"Hear me out. Hank and I each got a gun. I'll make sure you two are covered."

"Why are we even doing this?" The words spilled out of my mouth before I could put them back inside. I expected everyone to ridicule me, except maybe Bryan, but only Tony spoke up.

"Hey, man, what happened to you? You used to be all about a little adventure."

"I could be asking you the same thing," I said. "Adventure's one thing, but this . . . hunting animals illegally . . . dangerous animals at that . . . this is just nuts."

More howling filled the air. The mournful, bestial chorus silenced me. We all glanced around frantically. All of us but Tony. I thought my wondering was more than valid. Something must have happened to him too, for him to want to test himself like this. I couldn't imagine what it might be. The man had everything, yet here he was chasing one of nature's most vicious creatures, a whole pack of them by the sound of it.

I tried to imagine being somewhere else, and it almost worked. It almost worked, but then I remembered why *I'd* come up here in the first place. I needed to get away from the day-to-day, from me, from the weak worm of a man who'd let his ex-wife take his little boy away. As if by fucking her personal trainer she hadn't emasculated me enough. Fucking bitch. That was why I was here. I couldn't speak for the others, but it had to be for similar reasons. At the very least, we had in common the hope of escaping our confinement. Even Bryan, out of the closet almost a decade now, had to be caged somehow by something. Every man living in society was, if you believed Thoreau. Maybe Tony saw the thrill of the hunt as a way of freeing himself from modern life's shackles. As our leader—and whether we'd elected him or not, I think we had an understanding he was our leader—maybe I needed to trust him. Maybe we all needed to, especially now if the wolves were onto us. As if to remind me, they howled again.

"All right," I said. "I'll go with Tony."

The corner of his mouth twitched upwards.

He nodded at me. "My man."
I followed him into the dark.

The cacophonous chirping of crickets started up again. I couldn't decide if it was better or worse that I was sober. I assumed the latter. Tension held every last one of my muscles. Even deep breaths of the clean air didn't soothe my anxiety. The darkness around us was complete.

"Haven't heard a wolf in a while," I said in hopes of persuading Tony to head back to camp. I hated the tremor in my voice. Hoped he wouldn't notice it.

"Maybe they're scared of something."

"Like what?" As far as I knew, they had no natural predator. Maybe he was alluding to my own fear. Letting me know he heard it.

"Like us."

"Yeah, right."

"No, really. They aren't stupid. They know what this gun can do."

I couldn't help but laugh at that. He turned to me, frowning.

"You know how crazy you sound, right?" I said with a nervous giggle.

"Something about the wilderness brings it out in a man, don't you think?"

"Funny, I was thinking about that earlier." My voice had leveled out.

"Yeah?"

"Yeah. I mean, well, sort of. About the animal in man and whether or not it's a good thing that life's demands keep it . . ."

"On a leash?"

"Exactly."

"What do you think?"

"I don't know. I mean, in class, I've made the argument it wasn't such a good thing. That society and so-called civilized life keeps our true selves contained. That it's contrary to actual freedom, and maybe that's true, but I don't know. A pussy like me probably wouldn't last long in the wilderness."

"You'd be surprised, man."

"How do you figure?"

Leaves rustled. Not too close, but not too far either. Tony kept facing forward, gun pointed into the black ahead. His expression reminded me of the time I'd seen him fight. One of his teammates got too handsy with a girl at a party.

Tony stepped in. His buddy shoved him, and something switched in Tony's eyes. They went cold, almost lifeless. He knocked the other guy out with one punch. Seeing that same iciness did nothing to ease my tension.

"A friend of mine used to train fighters," Tony said, pulling me out of the memory. "Said one of his toughest students was a little White boy. Hundred ten pounds soaking wet. Total animal in the ring."

"Huh. Crazy."

My voice sounded small, almost childlike. Dwarfed by the darkness around us. Somehow, Tony seemed larger than life. I remembered all the times we'd raced. Sometimes he beat me; other times I beat him. The only constants were our friendship and that, each time, the victor didn't win by much. Often, victory only became clear in the race's final seconds. I didn't feel that way now. I felt instead I'd come to an imaginary finish line a long time ago but Tony had kept on running, gaining more and more ground, somehow growing stronger with every stride. Reward after reward awaited him at various intervals. I wasn't jealous. He'd busted his ass. Instead, I wondered where the fuck I went wrong.

More movement in the leaves ahead. A twig snapped. It was a hollow but resonant sound. These sounds were much closer than before.

"Can you see anything?" I whispered.

Tony shook his head. I shone my flashlight toward the noise. The illumination only made the foliage a lighter gray than before. My bladder felt full again, but I didn't want to stop because that would only drag this out longer, and God, I wanted so badly to go back to the tent and maybe to go home altogether, but I wasn't sure if I had a home anymore because Ayla had taken Wiley away and I was sick of my job and I doubted I could write another book and I just wanted to get laid so for a moment, however brief, I could feel alive again, but the rest of the time, I wanted to be too drunk to feel.

I shook my head of the rambling thoughts. I, or whoever was speaking in my head, sounded like an angst-riddled teenager. No wonder my life was in such a sorry state.

"You good?" Tony asked. "You're shaking that flashlight."

I looked down at my hand, which was indeed trembling. I willed it to stop.

Wiley. Wiley, please, whatever your bitch mother says, don't forget me. Don't forget I love you. Don't forget I was a good father, even if I came up short as a husband. Please.

More movement up ahead. Closer.

I couldn't take this. I wanted to turn and run. My bladder felt stretched to capacity. I thought if I moved at all, I'd piss. Fuck, I'd never hear the end of that.

Another howl tore through the night. It sounded harsher than all the ones preceding it. I inferred all sorts of feelings in its tone. Pain. Rage. Grief. Most frightening of all, I thought it held a human quality, which had to be my imagination. Following the sound, whatever had moved in the foliage ahead moved again, this time much faster. It was headed toward that awful howl. I turned the flashlight toward the scrambling. The beam fell on a clearing, and a pale shape staggered into its light and froze.

The woman was filthy. Dressed in rags. Legs unshaven. Hair in knots. Face caked with mud.

Emaciated. She faced us. Her wide eyes shone silver in the light. We stared at her. She stared at us. Tony lowered his rifle. I kept the flashlight on her, but my hand was shaking again. A small wet spot had formed on the front of my jeans. Turned out I did pee a little. Damn it.

The three of us stood in silence, watching each other, waiting to see who made the first move and what that move would be. From somewhere far away, Hank screamed.

The woman ran toward the scream, and we followed. I couldn't tell you what Tony was thinking. I didn't even know what I was thinking. We just ran after her. Pushing through low-hanging branches. Jumping over roots and stones. It was like we were racing again. Only I wasn't in as good of shape as I used to be. The mountain air, once so clean and refreshing, now felt harsh and cold as it tore its way down my throat, in and out of my lungs. Sweat poured into my eyes, blurring my vision. Through this, I thought I saw some sort of weapon in the woman's hand. A hatchet, maybe. No, I thought, couldn't be.

Hank screamed again, and Bryan screamed too. A loud report from the other rifle shredded the air. And then Bryan was calling our names. Calling for help.

"You hear that shit?" Tony said.

"Yes," I huffed.

"Hey, we're coming!" Tony hollered.

"Hurry!" Bryan again.

Up ahead, the woman pushed on. She seemed tireless. I didn't know how much longer I could go on. Even Tony was huffing and puffing now. Wounds glistened on his toned arms from where branches had scratched him. The left side of my abdomen started to burn. It felt like someone had stabbed me there with a hot knife. I wasn't sure what I'd do first: throw up or pass out. I was going to do one or the other, maybe both, if we didn't stop running soon.

Hank stopped screaming. Bryan wailed. Dread turned my legs to stone. Panic fluttered in my guts like a butterfly on meth. I wanted to turn and run the other way. I didn't want to see whatever awaited us up ahead. But Tony kept running, so I kept running too.

The woman dived through a thick patch

of foliage. We followed. Tony grunted and I yelped as we pushed through stabbing, scratching twigs. I prayed none of the leaves were poison ivy. Finally, we fell through the final stretch of bramble and into a clearing. What I saw brought no relief.

Hank was lying on the stony path. He had a chunk torn out of his shoulder. Bryan had removed his shirt and was pressing it to the wound. The white shirt was already soaked. It had turned completely crimson. Hank's face was very pale. His eyes streamed, tears running into his beard. When Bryan saw the woman, he blinked several times, as if he couldn't believe his eyes. I supposed he couldn't. All of this had become beyond belief.

"Where?" the woman asked.

"What?!"

Bryan spoke shrilly. Confused. Hysterical. Like we all were.

"Where did he go?" she asked.

"Who?"

"The one who did this."

"It wasn't any *he*," Bryan said. "It was some kind of . . ."

"Wolf," she said. "I know. I have to go after him."

"Now, wait a minute," Tony said. "The only thing we need to do is get my friend some help. We're in the middle of nowhere, and he's bleeding to death."

"It might be best if he did," she said.

"What?!" I think we all screamed that.

"Never mind." She looked at Bryan. "Which way did he go?"

Bryan pointed a shaky finger into the surrounding darkness. The woman moved to run in that direction, but Tony caught her by the elbow.

"Wait a damn minute. First, I think you owe us an explanation."

She jerked her arm away.

"How do you figure I owe you anything?"

"I figure whatever you're after took a chunk out of my friend's arm."

"Fuck you." She spat in his face and marched toward the place Bryan had pointed.

This time I caught her. I grabbed her from behind, around her waist.

She squirmed against me. "Let me go!"

"Just hang on, okay?" I said. "We need to get my friend some medical attention, and you . . . you don't look like you're in any shape to go off chasing wolves."

She started to relax in my arms. I didn't let her go. She hadn't earned my trust.

"Anyone bring their phone?" Tony asked.

"Mine's back at camp," Bryan said.

"Mine too," Hank said through gritted teeth.

Tony nodded in my direction. I shook my head.

"All right," he said. "We head back to camp. Bryan and I will help Hank." He looked at me. "Don't let this one out of your sight."

"You can let me go. I'm not gonna run," the woman said. "He's probably too far off for me to catch up to him by now."

"Why do you keep saying 'he'?" Tony asked. "It's a wolf, right? Just an animal."

Her jaw tightened. She looked down.

"He's my son," she said.

Tony and I exchanged glances. I loosened my hold on her but didn't release her completely. I was testing her. Had to see if she'd try to break free. Except for her labored breathing, she remained still.

"Your son is a wolf?" Tony said, shooting me another look, one that said, *This bitch is crazy.*

"It's a long story."

"Yeah, well, I'd like to hear it. I think you should come back to camp with us."

"You wouldn't believe a word I say."

Tony took the gun Hank was using and tossed it my way. I caught it with one hand. The woman didn't try to escape.

"All the same," Tony said. "You look like you could use some food. Some sleep. Maybe a bath."

The mention of her unwashed state made me aware of her smell. It was like wet dirt mixed with blood and body odor. Still, I found myself wanting her. I couldn't explain why, and part of me felt gross about it. Another part told me it was perfectly natural. Biology. The thrill of the hunt.

She wriggled out of my one-armed grasp and stood between Tony and me. She held up her hatchet. Tony and Bryan helped Hank to his feet.

"You said you have food?" she asked.

"Yes," Tony said.

"All right. I'll come back to your camp. Just don't expect me to stick around if someone comes to rescue us." Her gaze traced the gleaming curve of her hatchet. "I've still got a job to do." Now she looked back at me. "And if any of you tries to rape me, this hatchet's going in your groin."

We hiked back to camp. We considered hiking back down Moon Mountain to drive Hank to the hospital, but we figured he'd need attention quicker. Maybe someone could send a helicopter up here. Airlift him. None of our phones worked.

Bryan dressed Hank's wound the best he could. Tony stood watch at the edge of camp. I found the woman some clothes: sweat pants and a tank top. She thanked me and got dressed. I brought her a tin of sardines, and she ate with grotesque enthusiasm. Of course, I didn't blame her. She looked like she'd been living on nothing but nuts and berries and maybe even crickets for months. I offered her a packet of wet wipes. She took a handful of them, scrubbed her hairy armpits, and reached inside her pants to scrub her crotch. She went to hand them back to me, but I shook my head and pointed to the fire pit. She threw the now black and yellow wipes into the ashen remains.

Seeing the white and gray log shards got me thinking about building another fire. I set to work while the others watched. Hank was sitting up now. Some color had returned to his face. Bryan used wet wipes to clean his hands. Tony kept his eyes toward the darkness. The rifle rested on his shoulder. More wolves howled in the surrounding forest, but none sounded as awful or unnatural as the bellow of the beast that had undoubtedly injured Hank. The wolf this strange woman said was her son.

When the fire was built, I sat down next to her. Bryan sat next to Hank. Finally, Tony abandoned his post and joined us. He laid his rifle across his lap and kept his hand near the trigger guard. When we all seemed a lot more settled, I asked the woman to tell us her long story. I can only speak for myself, but I think we all wanted some answers. Here's what she said.

Wolf Mother

My name is Luca Barath, and eight years ago, I gave birth to a monster. For the past year, I've been wandering this wilderness, trying to kill my child. It would take little effort for him to kill me. I suspect he'd rather not because I am, after all, his mother. To know he's still capable of such love makes what I must do infinitely more difficult. And make no mistake: for reasons that will soon become apparent, I *must* do this. Chief among them is that I am his mother. He's my responsibility.

This tragedy, my tragedy, began with the miscarriages. Five of them. Five fucking babies I couldn't carry to term. You'd think after so many instances of watching your underdeveloped child flushed down the toilet, you'd be unable to feel anything. If only that were true. Every time another fetus left me as a lumpy, bloody mess of wasted potential, another place inside me tore open, left me with another scar. The worst part about it was it was all me. My husband's sperm was fine. Something was wrong with me. Some kind of uterine abnormality.

I so badly wanted a baby. Richard so badly wanted a baby. Do you know how terrible it is to know the person you love more than anything in the world wants something you feel like you're supposed to give them but you can't give it to them? It's the most awful feeling you can imagine. The depression and feelings of inadequacy were crushing.

I turned to booze and pills to numb the pain. And they worked sometimes. Unless I stayed up too late and a powerful rage took hold. I lashed out at Richard. Told him he was putting undue pressure on me. Told him to knock up one of the neighborhood girls if that would make him happy. I always woke up in tears, of course, and feeling like a hydrogen bomb had gone off in my head. On one of these mornings, Richard told me to go to rehab and said he'd leave if I didn't. I went but made sure he knew I was going grudgingly. Mount Sinai Rehabilitation Facility was the name of the place. It's still there, I'm sure. While I was a patient, I met a man who changed everything for me. But not in the way you'd think. His name was Cort Boggs, and he smelled like fire.

Something about this man staying in the same facility as me for reasons he didn't disclose made me disclose everything to him. To this day, I still don't know why. I guess, given what follows, it isn't too much of a stretch to attribute this magnetism to some kind of magic. Regardless of the reason, I told him everything, even stuff I refused to share in group. For instance, I told him why methods like adoption and a surrogate weren't options for me. That was because of my father. I came from money, but I married for love. Dad said that unless I bore him a child, I'd never see a dime of my inheritance.

I suppose I could have defied him and figured out the money later. Unfortunately, because of all my medical bills, I wasn't in any position to throw away the possibility of receiving such a significant sum of money. Richard and I were working class. Barely above the poverty line. Call me a hopeless romantic, but I thought marrying for love mattered.

My father kept on living.

The collection calls kept on coming.

My habits got more expensive.

By the time I met Cort Boggs, I was desperate. I even told him how desperate I was. I told him I would do anything to be able to have a child.

Now, I don't know if Boggs was the devil. I sure as hell didn't give him my soul. There was no contract for me to sign in blood. Nothing like that at all. Not even a verbal agreement. He simply told me what I could do, and I listened. I wrote down his instructions exactly as he gave them and followed them to the letter.

I know what you're thinking: *Here's the part of the story where she says she wishes she hadn't done it*. Right? That's the hell of it, though. I don't regret anything. I got what I wanted. I gave birth to a beautiful, blue-eyed baby. Not long afterwards, my father died and left me enough money to get out of debt and put a down payment on a three-bedroom dream house. For seven years, I got to be a mother to a sweet little boy.

But I'm getting ahead of myself. I should probably tell you how all this happened and how it all went horribly wrong.

My child, the one I now aim to kill, was conceived in the very same wilderness surrounding us. I came here to Moon Mountain after a thirty-six hour fast. I carried only a small bundle of wolfsbane, one vial of menstrual blood, another vial containing Richard's semen, a pound of raw hamburger, a lighter, a white candle, and a lock of hair from a little boy. When I reached the mountain's peak, I dug a pit, put the meat at the bottom, drizzled the blood and semen over it, wrapped the candle in the boy's hair, arranged the wolfsbane so it made a triangle around the hole, and lit the candle. And then I waited.

The candle burned down, sizzling strands of the hair. The wind blew, but the flame stayed strong. Wolves howled, but I didn't let them scare me. If I was to die out here, at least I'd have given my life in the effort of attaining something I so desperately wanted. When the fire ran out of wax and wick, it spread across the meat, enveloping it completely. I didn't think it was supposed to do that, at least not from a physics perspective. If I wasn't convinced then I'd stepped out of the realm of known science, the flame rising as a crimson column before me made it fact. The fire took the shape of a large wolf, red-orange with black eyes. Part of me wanted to run, but I'd already come so far, and I needed whatever this demon could offer me.

Its fiery limbs enshrouded me. The heat was intense, but somehow, my skin didn't burn. The wolf demon lowered me to my back. Its member penetrated me, even though I was wearing pants. I don't know how it was possible, but again, this was beyond science.

The wolf demon and I fucked all night. I don't know how the fire kept burning or how my stamina remained so tireless. All I know is when we finished, it was morning and I was with child. I could feel a strange heat in my womb and knew it was growing and would continue to do so. There would be no miscarriages this time.

Throughout the pregnancy, I had awful dreams. Giving birth to a fire that consumed me and Richard and all the nurses. Giving birth to a wolf cub that tore its way out of my stomach. Giving birth to the devil incarnate. I'm not religious. Still, the fear felt very real, very possible. I awaited my child's birth with excitement and dread. The shift between these emotions was cruel in its inconsistency. I often thought of dying.

Jonathan Winstead Barath was born at 11:31 on the evening of March 16, 2010. Until I laid eyes on him, I continued to harbor fears he wouldn't be normal. Even as I pushed, sweat soaking my hairline, a feeling like tiny claws tearing me apart from the inside, over the encouraging words of Richard and my doctor, I imagined something monstrous ripping its way out of my vagina, shredding my walls, splitting me end to end, feeding on me as I bled to death and Richard watched in horror, the doctor and nurses powerless to do anything. Should such an awful scenario have occurred, it would've destroyed Richard. I didn't want that. I feared what it would do to him more than what would happen to me. I was the one who dabbled in weird wolf magic. Richard was blameless.

The slick, crying baby the doctor pulled from me was no monster. Or at least, he wasn't yet a monster. Or, if he was, the bestial urges lay dormant and deep. No, on that day, he was a perfectly normal, healthy, painfully beautiful baby boy. I experienced true love at first sight.

I see the way you're all looking at me. *How can she sit here telling this story without bursting into tears?* The truth is not that I've no tears left, as you may suspect. No, it's that no amount of tears or any sort of outward display of grief can properly express what I feel. Instead, a storm of grief churns inside me. It will not dissipate until I die, and I cannot die until he does.

The years passed, and I won't tell you everything was picture perfect. We struggled as a family, with raising a child. I know now all those struggles were normal. Back then, I didn't feel so sure. Every toddler meltdown, every act of defiance, every type of antiauthoritarian behavior all kids exhibit, I worried that *now*, now I'd see the transformation into the monster I feared he'd always become. But then, not an hour later, he'd be docile. He'd tell us he loved us. He'd play nicely with others. Want to be with us. Miss us. All normal things. All wonderful things.

I've called this story a tragedy. In every tragedy, the central character has a flaw, something that makes their whole world fall apart. Supposing this is a tragedy, my flaw was only my total love for Jonathan. My love blinded me when I should've seen the danger right away. Not a week or two after his seventh birthday, the first neighborhood kid was killed. Torn to pieces. The morning after it happened, I knew something was wrong with Jonathan, though I wasn't sure what. He looked and acted tired, like he hadn't slept at all. Moved slowly. Yawned a lot. Sported black bags under his eyes. Another peculiar thing was that his pajamas lay discarded in the corner of his room. He lay in bed naked.

After the dead child was discovered, a creeping suspicion made me draw connections, but my love smothered them into silence. Jonathan didn't change every full moon. If that had been the case, I likely would've stayed ignorant unless he made some sort of mistake that led the police to him. Maybe even then. No, it happened a lot more frequently. It happened whenever the dormant beast got hungry.

I finally allowed for the possibility Jonathan might be responsible for these murders after three children died. On each of those following mornings, he exhibited the same exhaustion, a look of dishevelment, and had taken off his clothes. He lost interest in food, except for meat, which he always asked for undercooked.

I started checking on him nightly at two-hour intervals. I hardly slept myself. Richard said I was crazy. He, of course, didn't know *why* I was doing these checks. I told him I was afraid Jonathan would wander out and get murdered himself or the killer would break in. He asked me over and over if I was using again. He didn't know the truth. He still doesn't. As far as Richard knows, his wife and son are long dead. Maybe he isn't so far off.

One night in July, my worst fear finally came true. When I went to check on Jonathan a little after two o'clock, he wasn't in his bed. The scream tore itself from my lungs before I even knew it was coming. Richard rushed in. Asked what was wrong. Gasped when he saw the empty bed.

"Where is he?" he asked.

"Stay here," I said. "I'm gonna go out looking."

"We should go together," he said.

"No. Someone has to be here if he comes back."

He agreed and sat down on Jonathan's bed, looking down at his hands and probably feeling useless. In truth, I felt like he was. I loved him—I still do—but this has always been my fight.

I drove frantically through the neighborhood, my head on a swivel, nearly crashing several times into parked cars. I even almost ran over a scurrying raccoon. The fact no one called the police on me is astounding. A speeding vehicle, circling the neighborhood and swerving. It was too dark for anyone to recognize the car as their neighbor's. Probably seemed like I was casing the place, or lost and very drunk.

Damn near two hours passed. During the second hour, Richard started blowing up my phone like a jealous ex-boyfriend. I ended up switching it off. At no point did it occur to me Jonathan had come home. He couldn't have.

I parked at the edge of a patch of woods and got out. I switched my phone back on to use the flashlight but kept it silenced. The overgrown path wove through trees impossibly tall, impossibly dense. A rich stench of foliage choked the cold air. I hugged my arms to my chest. A heavy dragging sound from the surrounding woods drew my attention. I shone my light in its direction and immediately wished I hadn't.

A nightmare version of my son, something between wolf and boy, with an upturned snout, a shaggy brown beard and mane, and pointed ears, was squatting over another boy. The victim's throat was torn open. The Adam's apple gleamed white at the center of a red, ragged hole. Blood from the wound dripped from Jonathan's beard and lips as he cradled the boy's head. He lifted his gaze to me, and his pale blue eyes softened. The sight of his mother filled him with tremendous regret and shame. At least, that's how I interpreted it. Maybe it was only what I hoped.

He dropped the boy's head, and it landed with a wet thud. The dead face turned toward me upon impact. Its vacant eyes stared without sight. A lump lodged itself in my throat. I could do nothing but stare.

Jonathan stood, at least a head taller than the boy I knew. Patches of fur covered his lean physique. He looked much older than seven, but I recognized him just the same. He kept his eyes on me. I expected him to attack. Wanted him to. Instead, he ran away. I found my voice and called his name, but it was far too late. He was gone. I was alone. I called the police.

I, of course, said nothing about wolf boys or sexual liaisons with demons. I simply reported the body and said my son was missing. The police asked what felt like a million questions. Neither Richard nor I got any sleep that night. The morning light brought me no comfort. Instead, it made my nightmare seem far more real. During the night, I still harbored hope it was all no more than a bad dream. In the daylight, I could deny nothing.

A month of terrible depression followed. I often thought of using again. I came pretty close a few times, but ultimately, I decided to stay sober. My son deserved a mother who would let herself feel the full brunt of her grief. Two more children were killed. I knew Jonathan was responsible, but I kept silent. At some point, he'd come home. I hoped for and dreaded this.

Jonathan came back to me one afternoon I happened to have off from work. He didn't come to the door. I'm not even sure how he got in. He walked in on me in the kitchen while I was drinking coffee that had gone cold. I didn't spit the sip I'd just taken out in surprise like people do in the movies. I simply held it in my mouth as I gazed at the prodigal son.

"Hello, Mother," he said. I couldn't find the

words to respond. "I know what you saw, and I know what you know. I also know what you did to make me."

I swallowed, opened my mouth, but still couldn't speak. Emotions and questions overwhelmed me. I felt tremendous relief and heartbreak. I wondered where he'd been when not killing other children. How he was able to speak like someone much older. How he knew the ugly secret of his conception. I could voice none of these things. I could only stare at him through eyes blurred by tears.

He told me he'd been to the mountains. He said he knew what he did was wrong and tried to live alone, feeding on deer and game instead. Eventually, the loneliness became too much, and he returned. I found my voice and asked how I could help him. Vowed I would do anything to ease his pain.

"I want a family," he said, and I got the awful notion he meant to rape me.

Instead, he told me to call on the wolf demon again, using Boggs's spell.

"I merely want a companion. A sibling or lover, someone with whom I can share my life.

When you've given me that, I'll go away, and I'll never harm another child."

"I don't want you to go away," I said.

"But I must, Mother. You know as well as I that I do not belong here."

"Yes, you do. We're family. We'll make it work."

"No," he said, shaking his head. "I've told you what must be done. If you are not with child by this time next month, I will kill again, and I will keep killing until you give me what I've asked for."

"Why can't you find someone else?" I asked, already knowing the answer.

"You're my mother. I'm your responsibility. Do this one final thing for me."

I held out my arms, needing to feel him so badly it nearly burned. His features softened, and I thought, hoped, he meant to embrace me. Instead, he turned away and left me with a terrible emptiness.

I went back to Moon Mountain. I took my candle, menstrual blood, raw meat, semen, hair, and wolfsbane. I completed the ritual exactly as I had before. I mention this because it seems only by some cruel chance or the malevolent will of the forces I'd conjured that things did not go as they previously had. This time, it was much worse.

After another all-night fuck marathon with the wolf demon, I staggered down the mountain as the rising sun filled the sky with something like fire. The sharp pains in my stomach came before I even made it out of the wilderness. They were so bad, I cried out, doubled over, and dropped to my knees. My belly swelled up, lifting my shirt, the skin stretching taut before my eyes. The pain was exquisite, and I kept crying, but no one came to my aid. I don't think anyone was even around to hear. I felt like my insides were about to explode.

Most of the pressure forced itself downward. I was going to give birth.

I dropped my pants and stayed on my hands and knees. With my eyes pinched shut, I pushed. There was no epidural to numb the agony this time. I screamed as my uterus shredded, as my cunt spread, as blood and amniotic muck spattered the dirt, as, one-by-one, fucking *puppies* dropped out of me. Goddamn six of them. I collapsed when I was finished. Their cries were a cacophony of pitiful suffering. I turned and saw them: horrid half-lupine babies twitching and wailing in a black, lumpy puddle.

I don't know what came over me then. I just knew these monstrosities, these abominations, could not be allowed to live. Using what little strength I had, I found the nearest large rock. One after the other, I smashed my offspring, grunting with exertion, nearly vomiting at the crunching of tiny bones and the spray of more blood. When it was finished, I collapsed again. This time, I lay among the mangled and mashed remains of my children and bellowed.

Hunt

"And that was when he came out of the woods," Luca said. "My son watched me smash the life out of his siblings. He stood over me and said anything that happens from now on would be my fault. The blood of children, not just the brutally aborted half-wolf infants, would be on my hands.

"Since recovering, I've managed to keep him mostly to these woods, though sometimes he gets past me. I admit I've had opportunities to kill him, but something has always held me back. But I'm tired. It's time to end it forever. He must die."

She held up the hatchet, but her grip was loose. We all watched her, waiting for her to say more. All of us, that is, except for Hank. He was slumped over, exhausted. He didn't even perk up when she mentioned the name Cort Boggs. I thought for sure that'd get him going, but he remained sedate. Bryan kept suggesting Hank go to sleep, but Hank shook his head and shoved Bryan away every time.

Luca said no more. She threw the hatchet between her feet, and it stuck in the dirt. I considered, not for the first time, putting my arm around her. Holding her close and telling her it would be all right. After all, wasn't that what I was supposed to do? None of the other men showed any interest in consoling her. She didn't seem as though she wanted to be consoled. Her closed off posture and downcast eyes told the story of her isolation. How she didn't just expect this isolation to continue, but that she wanted it to continue. As she'd said, this was her fight.

It was a hard urge to ignore, though. Seemed the most natural thing in the world. Only, maybe it wasn't. Maybe this need to console each other—in particular, men's desire to console women—was some social construct. Solitude was natural. Solitude and survival. The only exception was when survival depended on cooperation. Sometimes, I felt like I was full of shit. This time was no exception.

When Luca said nothing else, Tony got up, shouldered his rifle, and walked back to the edge of camp. The howling had been sporadic while we listened to Luca's tale, and now it was almost nonexistent.

I turned to look at her. I examined her for any sign she wanted to let me in. Anything that said she didn't want to be alone. She gave no indication. She stared into the fire, probably thinking of monsters, but she could have been thinking of anything. Her walls were up. No one could bring them down or see through them, not even me. I thought about Ayla, about Wiley, about what the rest of my life would be like. I imagined seeing my kid on weekends, taking sexy students home on weeknights. At least for the first few years. Who knew what would happen later? After I got old and unattractive. After my kid grew to resent me as all kids grew to resent their parents. Shit, I didn't even know if I'd make it down from this fucking mountain.

Now, that was an odd thought. I wondered what brought it on. Luca's story, of course. It was ludicrous. Wolf demons, werewolf children. How gullible did she think we were? The only certainty as it related to Luca's story was she believed it. Maybe *she* was dangerous. Maybe she'd kill us all in our sleep. I looked at Tony. I had a feeling he wouldn't be sleeping at all. Maybe none of us would. Except maybe Hank.

Thinking of my old friend, now resting his head on Bryan's shoulder, made me extra shifty. We had to get him to a hospital first thing in the morning. We didn't even have to say it. I'm sure we all knew. God knew what kind of diseases that wolf carried. Or wolf boy. I shook my head and rolled my eyes. It drew Luca's attention.

"I wouldn't expect you to believe me," she said. "Any of you."

"Why would you say that?" I asked.

"It's a completely crazy story," she said.

"You can say that again," Bryan said.

"I swear it's true. Why else would I be out here?"

"I could think of a list of reasons."

"Ease off, Bryan," I said.

"What? We were all thinking it."

"I'm sure you were," she said. She turned her attention to the sleeping Hank. "You're gonna want to watch him closely."

"We'll get him to a hospital at dawn," Tony said over his shoulder.

"I don't think a hospital will do any good. If my son's a werewolf . . ."

"Look," Tony turned, "we've heard enough. He was bit by a wolf. That's all. And the wolf wasn't your son."

"It didn't look like a regular wolf," Bryan said, now inching away from Hank.

"Because it wasn't. I'm sorry I didn't make it to you in time."

Bryan, Luca, and I turned our attention back to the fire. Tony gazed into the dark woods. The howling persisted. It made me think of the old sound effects mixtapes I used to play on Halloween for Wiley. Even if Luca's story didn't contain a nugget of truth, it still affected me deeply. I feared who Wiley would grow up to be now that I wouldn't be in his life as much as before. I cursed Ayla for taking him away from me. My thoughts drifted to a dark place; I imagined strangling her in her sleep. Usually, when such thoughts surfaced, I shook them away and made myself focus on something else. Now, with the flames dancing before me, I dwelled on the awful image and the even more awful satisfaction it brought me.

Of course, killing her wouldn't help me get my son back. It would make things a lot worse. I'd get life in prison, maybe even the death penalty. Wiley would hate me forever. And would it even really be that satisfying? I suppose I would never know unless I tried, but that was one hell of a leap, one I couldn't envision myself taking. The idea of killing someone, even someone who had hurt me so profoundly, nauseated me. This was someone I'd loved, for fuck's sake! I now cursed myself for even entertaining the fantasy as long as I did.

Hank was lying on a log now. His eyes were closed. Drool leaked from the corner of his mouth. I thought he looked very peaceful. It didn't stop me from worrying, though.

There better not be any delay in the morning. We need to get him medical attention.

In the back of my mind, I heard Luca saying no hospital could help him. I hoped she wouldn't try to kill him in his sleep. He stirred, moaned, and licked his lips. Luca stared at him. I could only imagine what she was thinking. One hand dangled from her knee. It wouldn't take much for her to swipe the hatchet and bury it in his brain. I bet she was thinking the same thing. Her hand probably burned with need to hold the hatchet. The weapon had likely been the only thing to make her feel safe in the last year. While a year may not seem like a long time in our busy, hustle-and-bustle, civilized world, it probably passes like an eon out here, alone in the wilderness, on the hunt for your own flesh and blood.

Well, assuming everything she's said is true.

Not a second after I finished the thought, Hank pressed himself back up. He opened his eyes, revealing the blue eyes of a wolf. He opened his mouth, revealing massive, curved canines. Before anyone had a chance to scream, he bit into Bryan's throat and tore out a considerable fleshy chunk. Arterial spray followed, soaking Hank's face, painting it crimson. Bryan's eyes went dead, and he fell over, twitching.

Luca swiped for her hatchet, pulled it from the sand, and swung the weapon. Hank ducked the blow and scrambled for the surrounding woods. Tony spun, rifle aimed but his face slack with disbelief. His eyes were wide. His jaw worked, but he didn't speak. Hank turned to him, teeth bared and claws—fucking claws—raised, and half-howled, half-growled. Then he raced into the devouring darkness of the woods. I rushed to Bryan's side and cradled his head, even though it was much too late to help him. I sobbed uncontrollably and watched my falling tears mix with blood.

I haven't been completely honest with you. Maybe I should remedy that. Earlier in this manuscript, I made a passing reference to a homosexual experience I had when I was younger. I also said that after college, I found out Bryan was gay. While yes, he didn't come out of the closet to everyone until after college, I knew about his sexuality long before.

Throughout high school, I guess you could say I was curious. I definitely liked girls. All the porn I watched appealed to my male gaze. Sometimes, though, I wondered about guys. Bryan and I had been friends since elementary. Our parents had been friends and encouraged us playing together. I guess because I'd known him for so long, I had my suspicions about his sexuality. Sometimes I wondered what it'd be like to kiss him. Of course, I never made a move because, holy shit, what if I was wrong and he was as straight as Tony or Hank? I let all my reservations go during that party with the drama club my senior year.

If I'd told you this part of the story before I held my dead friend in my lap, I probably would've prefaced the tale by saying I consumed a fuck ton of alcohol that night. Now, I wasn't sober by any means, but to suggest I didn't know what I was doing wouldn't be fair to my friend's memory. So, yeah, I was buzzed, but not drunk. Even the buzz I had going was only so I could build the courage to broach the subject.

We ended up on the back patio, just he and I, reminiscing about the last few years and speculating on the future. He said he wouldn't be pursuing acting in college. Tech was where the money was, and he wanted to support himself. Maybe he'd join an amateur theater troupe one day, after he'd put down some roots. I wonder if he ever did. Talk of roots led to talk about marriage. I wasn't seeing anyone, but I got with the occasional girl at Tony's football parties. Bryan said he didn't see himself getting married.

With my tongue loosened by booze, I decided to ask.

"Well, you're gay, right?" I said.

"What? No."

"Come on, man. You can tell me. We've been friends forever."

"Please, you mostly just hang out with your jock buddies anymore."

"Ah, but I'm here now, right, bro?"

He sighed, stared ahead into the dark field of his backyard. "Fine. Yes. I'm gay, but I'm not out yet, so if you tell anyone . . ."

"I won't. I promise."

"Why's it matter anyway?"

Now, it was my turn to sigh. "Well, I guess,

I dunno. Ever since Cora and I broke up, I've been wondering what it was like to . . . be with a guy, and I figured, you being my friend and all . . ."

"How much did you have to drink?"

"I'm not that drunk. Besides, it's been on my mind for a while."

"All right, well, we should probably do whatever we're going to do away from the house. Don't want anyone to see."

"Yeah," I said, casting a glance back at the sliding glass door. "You're probably right."

We walked across the dark field to a patch of trees.

"So, what do you want to try?" he asked when we were obscured from view.

"I mean, I guess we could start with a kiss."

"Sure," he said.

For a couple of seconds, neither of us moved. Then he reached for me. His touch was delicate, not at all what I expected being touched by a man would be like. The back of my neck tingled under his fingers. His lips were every bit as soft as a woman's. It wasn't long before I felt myself growing hard. One of his hands drifted down there and lightly squeezed.

"Want a blowjob?" he asked.

"S-sure," I said, all of a sudden trembling.

"If you don't want to . . ."

"No, it's fine . . . just nervous is all."

"Relax," he said, going to his knees. "You'll enjoy it."

"Have you . . . before?"

"Once or twice," he said, winking at me as he undid my pants.

His hands were cool around my shaft, and I tensed. When he put me in his mouth, I practically melted into the tree behind me. The hot moisture behind his lips released all the tension I felt long before my orgasm came on. I'd gotten a few blowjobs before. Maybe I'd just gotten dealt a bad hand, but in my experience, high school girls used too much teeth. This was not the case with Bryan. He seemed to know exactly what I wanted. It was like a warm, wet massage on my cock. Not sure how long it took me to come, but it couldn't have been long. He swallowed too, which was something no one had done for me before either.

I dropped to my knees and embraced him.

And then I cried.

I know what you're thinking: it's 2018; being gay is no big deal. Just come out of the closet already.

For me, it isn't that simple. It's never been that simple. I still liked women. Do you know how hard it is to find a woman who's willing to date a man who's slept with another man? It's like finding a unicorn. Or at least that's how it's been for me. Ayla sure as shit wouldn't have been cool with it. She even said so herself once.

I was happy when Bryan came out. Part of me envied him.

Now, as I held his lifeless body in my arms, crying in front of him again—only this time he couldn't see me—I felt another void open up inside me. I felt bereft of a potential future, but most of all, I felt the need to wreak bloody, terrible vengeance.

I got to my feet. Glanced around for Hank's gun. When I found it, I marched over, picked it up, and racked it. Tony and I locked eyes. He nodded at me and turned to Luca.

"Where do these wolf people hang out?" he

asked.

"There's two now. There was just one, but I let your goddamn friend live."

"We'll fix that," I said.

"Our best course is to follow him. You take care of him. I'll take care of my boy."

Nods all around. We left the light of the fire behind.

The woods swallowed us. Our flashlight beams shone pitifully in the black. All around us, the crickets and toads created a Phil Spector-worthy wall of sound. Intermittent howls pierced through it. I squeezed the rifle so tightly my hands went numb. Sweat soaked the pits of my shirt and made my asshole itch. Despite my discomfort, despite the unpleasant buzz of my nerves, this wasn't like before. I didn't want to go back at all. This new mission, vengeance for Bryan, peace for Hank, would prove I'm a goddamn man.

I followed Tony. Somehow, he stayed cool as spring rain. He held his rifle in a relaxed grip. His features were hard, though, an intense, piercing gaze in his eyes. Luca held her hatchet at the ready. Her head turned every few steps.

She was on high alert. I had no idea how the rest of this night would go. I don't think any of us did. Could she do what needed to be done? Could *I*? I even had my doubts about Tony. This was all uncharted, even for a tough man like him, even for a long-suffering woman like her.

We came to a clearing at the bottom of a hill. Stones jutted out from dead leaves and dry pine needles like the crumbled remains of a castle. The moon and stars cast pale luminescence across the void and made everything silver, cold, lifeless. If not for the song of crickets and wolves or the cool breeze that carried the scent of pines, this would seem like a dead place.

At the center of the clearing, Tony stopped to look around. Luca and I joined him. The first growl came from on top of the hill. The beast that vocalized it had been behind us, and we hadn't even known. I wondered how long it had been there, how long death had loomed so close. We all turned toward the sound. No creature was yet visible. It was just too damn dark out.

Another growl came from somewhere beside

us.

"Was that the same wolf?" Tony asked.

"I don't know," Luca said.

Another growl.

"Are we fucking surrounded?" I said, my voice a harsh whisper.

"If we are, we'll deal with it," Tony said.

Luca raised her hatchet.

Another growl, closer. This came from the first wolf, the one atop the hill. Its eyes gleamed in the beam of my flashlight. It bared its teeth.

"Oh, shit," I said.

Tony turned, snarled.

"We should stand back-to-back," Luca said. "That way, nothing sneaks up on us."

"Good call," Tony said.

We did as Luca suggested. More eyes lit up in the surrounding darkness.

"This is bad," I said.

"Shut the fuck up, Walton. Don't be a pussy."

"Both of you, shut up."

The growling grew louder as the wolves came in closer. I could see them now. Silver fur that moved like sand dunes in the wind as the muscles beneath flexed. Even the crickets and toads had fallen silent now. It was as if all were watching this standoff. This confrontation between beast and man that would only end in fatality.

What was going to set things in motion? Which wolf would pounce first? Which human would fire off a shot or swing an axe? The chorus of growls added to the tension. Each growl was something bigger rumbling into life. Release had to come. But only bloodshed could bring it.

Tony fired the first shot. The slug tore a bloody chunk from the shoulder of the wolf on the hill. The wounded beast yelped. Another beast leapt. Tony turned toward it and fired. This shot proved more effective, blowing off the top of the pouncing wolf's head. The dead animal plopped onto the bed of fallen leaves and didn't move again. A third wolf attacked. This one's jaws clamped around Tony's forearm.

"Fuck!" Tony cried. "Goddamn it!"

Luca moved quickly. She pivoted and swatted the wolf across the snout with the flat side of her hatchet. It yelped and staggered off. Before it could attack again or retreat, I shoved Tony aside and shot the beast in the throat. Arterial spray showered the forest floor as the wolf danced the dance of the dying. I shot it again. It fell against a tree trunk and slid, lifeless, to the ground.

Something hit me hard, and I lost my footing. When I struck the ground, I lost my breath. And the gun. My vision blurred. I tasted blood. Something was on top of me, something big, pinning me to the earth. I didn't know if it was wolf or man or something in between. All I knew was naked fear. Without my breath, I couldn't scream. Under this weight, I couldn't move. Something hot blew against the back of my neck. Wet drops of saliva soaked the back of my shirt. Air returned to my lungs, but all I could do was blubber as blackness swallowed me.

Down the Mountain

I woke up surrounded by the dead and in a fuck ton of pain. It was nearly morning. A sliver of orange flared in the eastern sky. The starry purple was retreating slowly. Clouds of fog clung to the surrounding trees. The air stunk of copper and piss and loosened bowels. My left shoulder blade stung most of all, and my shirt around the injury was soaked with something sticky and warm. Luca and a wolf boy I assumed could only be Jonathan lay together in a tangle of bloody limbs. Her hatchet was buried in the side of his head. His hand, embedded in her chest. His closed eyes gave the illusion of peace despite the gory scene. Hers remained open and wide with terror of the void.

Several wolves lay about us. Some dead

from gunshot wounds. Others torn open and hemorrhaging steaming piles of guts. I became aware of wet chewing sounds, like an oversized wad of gum in the mouth of hell. I tried to reorient myself. Tried to push myself to my hands and knees. The exertion was too much, and I collapsed face-down again.

I managed to turn my head toward the awful chewing and almost vomited at the sight. Hank squatted among the shredded remains of Tony. My best friend's eyes stared sightlessly at me from his severed head. Hank had his mouth pressed to one of Tony's hands, eating it like fucking corn on the cob. Flecks of blood and ragged flaps of flesh fell between his hairy, clawed feet.

I had to get the fuck out of there.

Straining, I made my way to my hands and knees. Every muscle burned. I felt lightheaded. My breath came in and out in harsh, cool gasps. I pivoted and planted myself on my ass.

Hank turned to me and dropped Tony's mostly eaten hand. It landed with a sickening thump. He kept his teeth bared. Bloody drool fell from his heavily bearded chin. His eyes glowed that ghostly blue. The iciness of the stare stabbed into me like a knife left out in the snow. He stood. His pants had torn, and my gaze locked onto his massive, swinging wolf cock. That more than anything else made me panic.

I started sputtering pleas for mercy while simultaneously scanning the area for one of the rifles. He took a step forward, crinkling dead leaves. I scooted backwards, bumped a wolf corpse. My hand landed in a pile of guts. I gagged. Lifted my hand to look at it, now red and dripping with gristle. Hank took another step, this time snapping a twig.

Something in me snapped too. I lurched to my feet. Grunted against the exquisite pain.

Where are the fucking guns?!

Hank came closer. A low growl rumbled in his throat. His hot breath made steam in the cool morning. I swore I could smell it: whiskey, dog breath, and rotted meat. Wet dog and unwashed man. His hands stretched out before him as he advanced. Hooked claws like cactus spines. The big wolf dick swung with each step, slapping his inner thighs.

I finally spotted one of the guns.

Behind him.

Fuck.

I held up my hands in a gesture of surrender. "Hank, please. It's me."

He kept coming. Said nothing.

"Please, this isn't you. You've gotta fight it, man. Come on!"

His glowing wolf eyes narrowed into slits. He drew closer. So close now I could feel his goddamn body heat. A radiant cloud of foul humidity. Foul *humanity*. This wasn't some aberration, some anomaly of nature. This was Hank, the true Hank, the dormant beast, now awake, now hungry. I really needed to find that other gun.

A black and pink tongue licked across Hank's lips, across the points of his fangs.

"HANK!!!"

He was only a few paces from me now. He bent at the knees. Ready to pounce. Snarling, eyes burning, claws spread, and reared back. I was a fucking goner.

Then an idea hit me.

I reached for my wounded shoulder blade.

As I pressed my fingers into the wet wound, I determined it was indeed a bite mark. Whether wolf or wolf man, I didn't know, but I had to try something. I smeared a generous amount of blood on my hand and reached out.

"I'm just like you," I said. "I'm a beast. I've been bitten. We're the same!"

Hank cocked his head to the side like a confused dog. He loosened. He still made his way toward me but at a more tentative pace. He leaned forward and sniffed my fingers.

"See. That's it. That's a good boy. I'm like you. We're the same. You don't have to . . . eat me." With my other hand, I reached for the buck knife at my hip. "That's a good boy." I let him lick the blood from my fingertips, then moved my hand to scratch behind his now pointed, leathery ear. He closed his eyes and leaned into the caress. "Yeah, see? That's right. It's okay."

I unsheathed the knife with a quickness I no longer thought myself capable of. He opened his eyes and snarled. Before he could bite my extended forearm, I rammed the blade under his chin. He gurgled and whined as hot blood spilled over my knife hand and pattered the ground between us. I shoved him away, removing the knife as I did so. He took three shaky steps backwards and collapsed in a heap.

The sky was nearly half-orange now. I turned back toward camp. While I ran, I kept the knife clutched tightly and pointed ahead. Ready to kill anything that got too close. Or die trying.

I returned to camp and scared several carrion birds away from Bryan's corpse. One of his eyes was gone. The wound on his throat had been widened. Flies crawled and buzzed about him. They didn't scare as easily as the birds. I considered burying him. No time. The fire had gone out, so that was no use either. I had no choice but to leave him there. The birds would come back. I hoped there would be something left of him when the authorities came. Of course, I thought I might not even call anyone. I didn't know how to even begin explaining what happened. Save for writing it down, of course.

I gathered up some jerky and nuts and dried fruit, some water, and my notebook. I put it all in my backpack. I changed my clothes and did my best to clean myself up. When I felt I had everything I needed, I scoured the area for Tony's keys and hiked back down Moon Mountain, alone and in pain. Pointing the knife at shadows and sounds brought me brief moments of solace. But eventually, with only a third of the way to go, I tossed it away without a second thought. Something told me I wouldn't need it.

I reached the RV and leaned against it, pressing my forehead against the warm metal body. My breath slowed, grew steady. The bite on my shoulder blade didn't even hurt anymore.

I drove Tony's RV to the outskirts of Paradise, parked it, and walked into town. I found a diner with chrome trim and dirty windows and booths that had housed some infinite amount of butts. The aroma of burnt coffee hung about the inside. Coffee sounded nice.

A blonde server with thick foundation and long, pink fingernails escorted me to a booth and handed me a menu. Not even ninety seconds later, she brought me black coffee. I ordered a hamburger and took out my notebook to start writing this manuscript you're now reading.

After Pink Fingernails poured me a refill on coffee, someone else walked through the door. The smell of a campfire clung to this newcomer so strongly it drew my attention to him. He dressed in a shiny, expensive looking suit. He had black hair, slicked back, and a white face so smooth it seemed he never had to shave. When he saw me, he grinned, and a ball of lead filled my stomach.

He told Pink Fingernails he was here with me and approached my table, and I didn't refute his claim as he slid in across from me. He ordered no food and no drink. He didn't even touch the ice water Pink Fingernails brought for him. We didn't speak. He'd say something when he was ready, and I would listen. I knew that so deeply, I offered him no greeting, only continued writing, stopping to sip coffee every few minutes.

When my burger came out, he leaned forward. He zeroed in on me as I dressed the bun with ketchup and mayonnaise. As I discarded the onion and tomato and lettuce. As I lifted the sandwich to my lips.

I took one bite and gagged. I spit the bite onto the plate and lowered the sandwich.

He was grinning at me again.

I crossed my arms and leaned back. I stared into his black eyes.

"You have something to say?" I asked.

He maintained his grin for a beat, then spoke.

"You know who I am. You've heard what I can do. You know I can give you anything."

"Anything, huh?"

"Anything. You can kill Ayla without laying a finger on her. Get your boy back. Sober up, even. You just have to ask me, Walton."

"There's a catch," I said. "There always is."

"You'll live your life knowing you did something monstrous."

I touched my wounded shoulder blade. "I think I may become a monster regardless."

"Then what's the risk?"

I stared at him long and hard. The fiery smell was oppressive now, like I'd leaned my face near a campfire. I considered Mr. Boggs's words very carefully. Imagined Ayla dying. Imagined our son returning to me. Sobriety didn't seem so bad either. For some reason, I'd lost all urges to drink. I could have my boy back. I wasn't crazy about sacrificing Ayla. It seemed cruel and maybe even unnecessary. Of course, who knew what would happen now with the wolf's blood running through me? How could I possibly return to normal life?

Pink Fingernails returned to the table.

"Are you gonna order anything?" she asked my well-dressed companion.

"I'm not sure yet."

With a subtle roll of her eyes, she looked at me. "Everything tasting okay, sir?"

I glanced down at my burger. I glanced at Mr. Boggs. "You know what? No. Not at all. I'm sorry. Here." I dug out a twenty and put it on the table. "I think I'll be moving on."

"Okay, you want change?"

"Keep it."

"Thank you." Everything about her brightened.

Cort Boggs watched me get up. As I turned, he said one final thing.

"You'll never get another chance," he said.

I didn't respond. I didn't even look back.

I intended on returning to the RV. Driving until I found a police or sheriff's station. But a rustling sound in an alley gave me pause. I turned and saw a raccoon digging in an overturned trashcan, eating the contents of a torn open bag. My own belly rumbled, and I realized how hungry I was. The well-done burger at the diner had made me gag, but something about a fresh kill, even a verminous beast like a raccoon, made me salivate.

I walked toward the creature. It didn't notice me. Only kept eating what looked like expired coleslaw. A growl started in my throat. I didn't even do it consciously.

I advanced on the creature, focused more on the hunt than on my hunger. I couldn't let my need distract me.

As I crept forward, I wondered what I'd do once I'd feasted. Once I'd fully embraced the animal. Shirked the man, the man who hadn't been much of a man to begin with.

The raccoon raised its face to me. Its black, cartoon criminal mask shadowed eyes filled with more curiosity than fear. It had nowhere to go. I was too close. *I will feed,* I thought. *And then I'll go home.*

Moon Mountain loomed ahead. The trees covering it swayed in the breeze. They seemed like a single great beast. A wolf-shaped cloud hovered over the snow-capped peak.

Yes. I'll go home.

Who is Lucas Mangum?

Award-nominated author of a dozen books, including the Digital Darkness series, Saint Sadist, and Gods of the Dark Web. Vaporwave Dad. You can join his newsletter at:

https://www.lucasmangum.com/

Made in the USA
Monee, IL
10 February 2024